A Generation of Lighted Evergreens

Episode Five
Orphan Dreamer Saga
A Novelette: Austin Cavanaugh

J. Nell Brown

ROGUE READS
LLC

BOOKS BY
J. Nell Brown

NONFICTION

Shhh, My Father Is Speaking, and I Am Listening: A Bible Study on Hearing God's Voice

Blood Moon—God's Warning: Why Knowledge of Jewish Feasts Is Essential to Understand the Blood Moons of 2014 and 2015

FICTION

Orphan Dreamer Saga
Orphan Dreamer and the Missing Arrowhead

Orphan Dreamer and the Glass Tattoo

She Laughs Last

Orphan Tree: Rooted in Eternal Love

Collector's First Edition Paperback
The Omega Journey: Blood Moons Whisper

COMING SOON

A Generation of Lighted Evergreens

Orphan Falls: Wild and Free

House Guest

Orphan Star: The Mark

Little Peach Lies

Orphan's Seed

If Love's a Fish

Orphan's Horizon

Orphan's End

1—SUGARCANE

12:00 P.M.
FRIDAY, AUGUST 11, 1967
BELLE GLADE, FLORIDA

AUSTIN CAVANAUGH HAD BEEN IN the same position for the last five hours—slightly hunched with a machete in his right hand, chopping sugarcane in a hot, humid field.

He laid the cutlass by his feet, dug in his pocket, and retrieved a gray-brown handkerchief, a Christmas gift from his father, who had been a peanut farmer. Dabbing his forehead, he soaked up droplets of sweat, a field hand's reminder that the old fireball didn't play favorites. "Whaddya say, 'bout time for some water, Chuck?"

"When the boss man says so." Chuck kept chopping down stalks of cane. He was Austin's local friend and had grown up in Gainesville, Florida, down the dirt road from Austin's father's peanut farm.

"Ain't no rest for the weary . . ." Austin's arm ached as he gripped the wooden handle of his machete, swiping the blade through another clump of thick cane.

"You ain't takin' a break without the whistle chirpin', are ya?" Riddled with the remnants of untreated pneumonia and asthma, Chuck hacked up strands of mustard-colored phlegm. The dirt and pollen hadn't helped his allergies or lung infection.

"Nope—just dreamin'."

"What about?"

"A cozy place in the country, a vegetable garden, a few chickens, a hammock, and a tall glass of ice-cold lemonade." Austin kneaded his wrist, easing the constant throb. "How's the pneumonia?"

"I ain't laid out yet. You'll know it's bad when I fall over dead."

"Don't want it to come to that. Will the doc see you?"

"He ain't never seen no colored people."

"But he takes care of sick people, don't he?"

"Yep."

"You're sick."

"You done died and gone to heaven. Yes, sirree." Chuck rocked back on his heels, his thumbs tucked beneath his blue suspenders. "You lost your mind somewhere in this cane field." As though stepping on a drumline, Chuck dipped to the right. "Go on wit yo bad self."

Austin gazed into the heavens. Closing his eyes, he allowed Florida's sun to bake his skin to a deeper brown. No need to keep the sun from doing her business. Brown was brown in the South. It didn't matter if you had one teaspoon of cream in your DNA or ten, so be proud of the Almighty's doing.

"Whatcha doin'?"

"Thinkin'."

"Oh, Lord . . ." Chuck's gaze skimmed over the cane field.

A channel of wind found its way between the stalks. Leaves slipped by each other, creating a fan.

Opening his eyes, Austin turned and stared down the wide dirt road that wound like a diamondback rattlesnake. The dirt and pebble path ended at the big house—a white, rectangular clapboard building adorned with black shutters and six twelve-pane windows. A deep wraparound porch encircled the boss's field house like his belt—low and dipping in the front. Austin knew about the belt because the boss had chased him down the road, threatening to use it.

The reason?

Austin's yellow lab, Gus, hadn't stayed put—the boss had found him down the main road, tucked beneath a shrub. Old Gus had probably spotted the shady boughs of the sugarcane field's lone oak tree and decided he needed a little more cool air, or he had mindlessly chased a squirrel, which gave him an excuse to track his master's scent. The reason hadn't mattered, and since then, Austin had shut Gus inside their wooden shack by the stream.

Hope he's not gone and fainted in that old shed. Couldn't bear to find him laid out from the heat.

Hunching low, Chuck tiptoed to Austin's side, breaking his thoughts. When Chuck grinned, a space the size of a man's thumb separated his dingy teeth—teeth like a black-top wedged between two dirty-white fishtail Cadillacs. A drunken brawl in the juke joint had claimed his missing teeth, but who was Austin to judge a man's past? He swept his machete across the bases of several stalks of cane, excising them with an executioner's accuracy.

One paycheck closer to a better life.

2—Dreamin's for Fools

A WHISTLE CHIRPED IN THE distance. "Water!" Austin slipped his machete inside a leather pouch that dangled from his belt.

The whistle meant lunchtime, but he would have to wait another five hours before he ate his usual dinner of peanut butter and bread. Neither required refrigeration. His shack didn't sport many amenities. Before going home, though, he would drop a few more coins into his pocket.

What else could a man ask for?

As he walked to the water hose, his mind wandered.

What else could a man ask for? A rose whose petals are made of velvet brown with a stem that consists of two long, slender legs. He chuckled at his romantic daydream.

It was a long shot.

"Glad the ol' man blew the whistle," Chuck said, "because I'm 'bout dried up."

In step, they trudged toward the water faucet. Even Austin's dishonorable discharge from the Navy for gross intoxication hadn't erased the memory of the chant: *left, left, left-right-left.* He paused and hung his head. How could a seventeen-year-old cope with war while drowning out the loud, mocking dark voices that haunted him after his mother's death?

At the watering hole—tin cups in hand—they waited at the end of a long line. The lone oak tree's boughs dipped low, almost sweeping the ground. A stingy wind blew through its leaves and provided some relief.

Austin scanned the base of the tree, looking for Gus. No clump of mangy yellow fur. His breath slowed with relief. After ten minutes, it was his turn to fill his cup. He slurped down the tepid water before filling it again.

"Got something to eat?" Chuck asked Austin as the field master opened a large bin.

"Savin' my appetite for dinner with Gus. You go on and eat."

Chuck retrieved his knapsack. "Don't mind if I do."

While Chuck ate a leftover chicken thigh, collards, and a piece of bread, Austin stared into the distance. *Don't look at the food, then you won't be hungry.* The problem lingered. He could smell the Southern-cooked meal, a Mrs. Chuck Jackson special.

Chuck licked his fingers, removing the last smears of grease and spices from his hand. "Whatcha thinkin' 'bout?"

"Love."

"The heat has done gone to your head. You think of some of the strangest things in these hot fields."

"Best place for dreams, and better than reality."

"Mrs. Jackson has a sister, but boy, she packs a hot temper."

Austin shook his head. "She's not right for me."

"You'll find the right one." Chuck thumped his friend across his shoulder. "Let's get back to work. The more we chop, the more coins in our pockets."

Did a heavenly hand turn up the sun's temperature gauge? Austin wondered. A volcanic heat blasted his skin, sapping out every drop of perspiration. His mouth dry, he tried to answer his friend, but his tongue refused to cooperate. Instead, it latched onto his palate and hung on.

Chuck stroked his chin. "Spit it out."

As they walked, Austin tipped his tin cup to his mouth, and the last drops of warm water fell between his lips. Hungry and ashamed, he tossed the cup into his satchel, buried his hands in his pockets, and focused on the tips of his dress shoes. *Better than bein' homeless on skid row, where folks would rather spit at you than give you a helpin' hand.* Only a poor workingman wore his best shoes to the fields Monday through Saturday and then polished them to a shine on Sunday for church. The wingtip shoes had started refusing to come to a shine about a month ago, and one of Austin's toes now protruded, revealing a dingy sock.

In a low voice, he shared his heart with his friend. "If-f-f love's a fish, she must be a pink salmon, swimmin' up a cold-water creek—troubled, tryin' somethin' mighty to find her intended." He looked at Chuck and then found the tips of his shoes again. "I may not have much—"

"You got that right—but neither do I. Sorry for interruptin'."

"It's okay. I . . . I want a missus."

"Well, you string words together real pretty," Chuck replied. "You could be one of those fancy poets once your probation's done. That'll get you a real classy lady."

"I'm talkin'—dreamin'. Nothing more."

"Go on wit yo bad self." If Chuck had been a cheerleader, those six words would have been the loser's ninth-inning cheer, meant to arouse confidence. "After you swim up that cold creek and meet the lovely lady, what's your plan?"

"Gus, the missus and me are gonna find a little house, and the missus is gonna have a baby girl." Austin grinned, revealing two missing teeth on the right side.

"Just like that?"

"Yep."

"No son?"

"A girl will do fine."

"Well, lookie here now, you've got a plan. That's for sure. Problem is, if the Almighty grants you one wish, you'll be wantin' another."

"Does the wantin' ever stop?"

"Nope, as long as you're amongst the livin' it gets worse, till you done gone plum mad, begging for the last inning to finish."

"It was the wantin' that ended me up on the chain gang." He shook his head.

"Austin, we been friends for a long time." Chuck fiddled with his handkerchief. "You got somethin' you wanna tell me?"

"Time to go back to work."

Back in the field, Chuck grabbed an armful of sugarcane and carried it ten feet, piling it with the other stalks. The truck for weighing and counting would arrive toward the end of the day. Chuck laid a tattered rag over his pile, ensuring no one would steal it and claim the pickings as his own. "I'm gonna be honest with you, Austin. Findin' a pretty girl and convincin' her to marry you is gonna be slipperier than salmon."

"Why?" Austin swung his machete, low and hard, severing another stalk of cane.

"You got a past."

"Don't everyone?"

"Yours sounds messy, and you're talking 'bout findin' a real lady and bringin' up a baby girl."

"But . . ."

"Don't know the details. Don't need to. What I do know is that the Navy don't send men home during a war. Even though we colored, the US Navy was draftin' men, not sendin' them back across the Atlantic—unless they were causin' trouble."

Austin's empty gut twisted into knots.

After a few moments, Chuck sang a soulful tune. "Swing low, sweet chariot, comin' for to carry me home . . ." He stopped his song and looked at Austin. "A past more scrambled than eggs. Burnt ones at that."

Emotion fought to creep into Austin's throat, but more than one occasion had taught him that crying wasn't an option. He was a man—only girls and women were allowed to cry. So he ignored his discomfort, bent over, and slid his hands down another stalk of cane, stripping it of leaves while peeling his callused hands raw.

A red liquid striped the last cane, and he watched his blood trickling down the stalk.

My little girl won't be shuckin' cane beneath no midday sun. She'll be a dreamer, livin' my dreams. He bent over, brandished his knife, and chopped another bunch of cane, ignoring the throbbing in his right hand. Sweat glued his shirt and pants to his body. *What a man wouldn't do for a cold glass of lemonade.*

Stripping leaves from stalks, he closed his eyes and traveled to his dreamworld—a place of freedom, peace, family, and happiness . . .

From his father's shack, Mother Rosa Lee hollers, "Austin, come onto the porch and drink some lemonade."

His legs carry him to the porch faster than the Pony Express— or at least his best version of a horse galloping at thirty-eight miles an hour. On the rotted porch, he clutches a glass of iced lemonade. Ice clanks against the mason jar as the drink swirls and dips around frozen cubes of water. Tart and sweet on his tongue, the beverage reminds him of his life. He tilts the jar, allowing the sweetness followed by the tartness to bathe his tongue . . .

"Austin!" Chuck's voice snatched Austin from his dreamworld.

His hands were moving slower than usual. "What's wrong?"

"Boss is comin'."

"Thanks." He bent over and swung, removing another stalk. *No water and definitely no lemonade.*

Seconds turned to minutes, and another hour passed. "Chuck," he said.

"Whatcha need?"

"What's the word when something ends up the opposite from what you'd expect—you know, like it comes across one way, but the reality is totally different?"

"Mmm . . . you mean irony?"

"Yeah, that's the one."

"Whatcha need it for?"

"My life . . ."

"What?" Chuck crinkled his brow.

"Lemonade's like my life."

Chuck shook his head. "Man, from salmon to lemonade. You done gone completely silly."

"The sour, I've lived it."

"And the sweet?"

"It's coming. Wait and see."

"I'm thinkin' that you is hungry. First you talkin' 'bout salmon and now lemonade."

"But I don't have neither."

"Keep on dreamin'." Chuck slapped his friend on the back. "And I'll be standin' beside you at the church."

Austin grinned. "Thanks." He shook Chuck's hand. "You're my friend. Always have been. Hope my baby girl finds a friend like you—another girl, of course."

"She may want a gentleman—a husband and children of her own."

"Nope." Austin shook his head as if the more violently it moved right and left, the more his assumptions would be right. "Don't want no man messin' with my little girl."

"You don't want her marryin' no woman, do ya?"

"Absolutely not." Austin glanced at his friend. "Okay—but only if I approve of him."

"Lordy. He won't know what hit his scrawny hips. What if she goes and finds herself one of them . . ." Chuck cupped his hands around his mouth, "white boys?"

Austin dropped his machete. Heat exploded inside his body. "Why'd you say a thing like that for?"

"Joking—passing the time."

"I like my coffee black. You?"

"Same way for my little Gertrude."

Another hour slipped away. Austin stretched his muscles and then dried his hands on his frayed cabana shirt. Looking at his palms, he noted the calluses and dirt lodged into the fissures of his rough skin. "My baby girl won't be a field hand. She's gonna have it real good, schoolin' and everything."

"Schoolin' costs money." Chuck shook his head. Fine leaves rustled. He hunched low, and Austin did the same. Chuck's eyes darted from left to right. "Best stop talkin' and get back to choppin', or the boss won't leave your hide intact to be havin' no children."

"It's 1967, not 1835."

"We had our turn in the state pen, and that means life is like the eighteen hundreds for you and me."

"I was a Navy man."

"Ain't nobody 'round here care about your military service. And don't you forget it. Hang low. Ya hear me?"

Austin nodded and went back to chopping, but his dream didn't die with his friend's tongue-lashing, just as his ancestors' dreams hadn't died with their overseers' whippings. He could dream big enough for himself and his baby girl, but she would be the one to live that dream. He smiled while the thoughts of fatherhood soothed his aching body.

Fear, hopelessness, or both? Chuck had been right—fools dreamed, and men toiled by the sweat of their brow.

3—The Bank

THE SUN DIPPED BEHIND THE big house, casting the clapboard abode in a tangerine glow. Its frosted windows looked haunted. No doubt centuries of ghosts hid within them, willing to tell their stories with a tap across the glass to those who possessed a keen sixth sense.

Austin didn't believe in ghosts.

He licked chapped lips, imagining the sweet nectar of a ripe tangerine. Labor and sweat hadn't tamed his imagination—it soared around, light as the feather on an eagle's wing. He swung low and chopped the last of the day's sugarcane.

Jeanette defined beautiful, and he'd noticed her last Sunday at church. A flowered yellow skirt had swayed atop long, mahogany legs as she strolled down the church aisle. When she smiled, her cheekbones rose high and her bright teeth flashed in contrast to the sanctuary's dim lighting.

A whistle ended Austin's daydream.

"Time to go home." Chuck sheathed his machete, and Austin sheathed his blade as well.

"You're grinning—you in love? You already met her, haven't you?" All in one gulp, his friend had discovered the secrets of Austin's heart.

Ignoring Chuck's questions, Austin strode toward the pebble road. Sweat soaked his shirt, pasting it to the curves of his back muscles.

Chuck chased after his friend. "How'd I miss the clues?"

"You ain't the sleuth you used to be."

"You done already snagged your lady." Chuck shoulder-bopped his friend, then wheezed and hacked until his lungs calmed.

"You need to go see the doc."

"Not possible. You reeled her in?"

"Haven't tried yet. Noticed her last Sunday."

"Now, I'm tellin' you right now." He leveled his finger at Austin. "We've got some time—got to collect our pay at the big house, and then I'll walk you to the split in the road. All the while, I want you to start talkin'. Hear me?"

"You sound like my pappy."

"Pappy or not, I'm all ears."

A pebble found its way into the tip of Austin's shoe. "Ouch!" He hopped on one foot, removed his shoe, and dumped the offender back onto the road.

"That's your punishment for keepin' a friend in the dark."

"Chuck, me and the good Lord have had our fair share of conversations on the matter."

"And the good Lord expects you to share."

"Not till I'm ready, and when the right time's . . . right."

They neared the house and stopped, waiting at the end of the line for their pay. Nervous, Austin shifted to one foot and then the other. What kind of mood would the beefy-faced man be in today?

His voice oscillated as though he was trying to find the right note. "Two Sundays ago, Pastor Butler asked this question—'Why are you here? You gonna suck up oxygen or get on about God's business?'"

"Did he hit the pulpit like usual?"

"No." Austin glanced at his callused hands—empty and waiting for thirty dollars—wondering about his own future. Emotion crept into his throat. *Don't show emotion.* But his body ignored his instruction, so he peeled the T-shirt from his chest and dried his face.

"It's gonna be alright, Austin. Go on wit—"

He raised his callused hand, letting Chuck know he didn't need to finish his mantra, then slipped his hand into his pocket—empty. *Can't feed and educate a baby girl on thirty dollars a week.*

The boss's white clapboard house sprawled behind a long metal table—the bank, the place sugarcane laborers received their week's wages. The boss stood behind the table. As usual, his belt struggled to hold up his pants. His face reddened to the color of a pomegranate as he screamed at a laborer who was about twenty men in front of Austin. The boss's jowls were stuffed with tobacco. Brown specks flew into the tawny face of Tibet, a Jamaican man trying to earn a living for his family of four back on the island.

"What's he so mad about all the time?" Austin asked.

"Got too much—it's plain rotted him from the inside out."

The foreman appeared calm. The wind tore into his silver hair, and he fanned through one-dollar bills, counting the man's wages.

How much? Austin thought as he listened to the foreman count out thirty dollars for six days' work. *That might buy ol' Tibet some milk, bread, and—for two dollars a day—a room inside one of the boss's concrete field shacks. Not much left for a wife and kids back home though.*

Austin's posture sagged, and bitterness filled his mouth. He stuffed his hands into his pockets to keep him from doing something stupid. Even if he earned his usual thirty-five, it wasn't enough to feed a wife and a baby girl, much less build a proper house for his two ladies and purchase a good education for his child.

He inched closer, waiting his turn and praying for at least forty dollars.

"What's her name?" asked Chuck.

"Jeanette."

"Pretty name."

"Thought so. She's as beautiful as her name." Jeanette's afro framed a lovely face, with a hint of red splashed beneath her mahogany skin. *Redbone*, the dark-skinned Southerners in their little Baptist church had called her.

Redbone, mahogany, he didn't care what they called her. She looked beautiful, and that was that. "Hope she's at the Sunday church meetin' or Wednesday prayer meetin'."

"Ask her out for ice cream."

"Don't have an icebox in the shed."

"Bring her to our place. We'll grab a stash of ice from our neighbor."

"You and your wife wouldn't be put out?"

"Friends help friends." Chuck grinned and moved closer to the bank. "We all gotta eat." He winked.

"My past's too messy." Warmth crept up his neck as he thought about his girl—well, she wasn't really his, at least not yet. He thought about her sitting in the third pew of their church with her ankles crossed.

"She ain't got no rough past, does she?"

"It ain't tainted like mine. The old church ladies told me so. She's smart, real smart—smarter than the foreman. Has a master's degree and teaches at a high school." He grinned sheepishly. "She's young too—'bout ten years younger than me."

"You's a cradle robber." Chuck playfully punched his friend's shoulder.

Churning up a trail of dust, a driver careened past the laborers in her Pontiac Tempest. The boss's daughter stopped the car and stepped out.

"What's she doin' here?" Chuck asked.

"I wouldn't let my baby girl come out in the field among all these men. The boss don't have control over her ways—does what she wants to."

Chuck nudged his friend. "Jeanette ain't like her—nose stuck up in the attic?"

"No sir, but she talks like them white girls, with words I don't even know the meanin' of, but I'll learn." Austin reached into his satchel and removed a little black book.

"Who gave that to ya? Ya steal it?"

"It's mine. See this?" Austin pointed to his name written in neat print in the front of the book. "Chap Max Jones gave it to me."

"Who's that?"

"Prison chaplain."

"Read something, we got another ten minutes. The boss ain't in no hurry. He'll keep us out here all day to shave a penny off our pay."

Smiling, Austin opened the little book to a random page. He sounded out the letters like Mrs. Thompson had showed him. She was the woman at church who'd helped him learn to read after he was released from prison.

"J-e-r-e-m-i-a-h."

"Jeremiah," Chuck glued the letters together, forming the word.

"Thanks." Austin struggled through the passage. "For I know the thoughts that I think toward you . . . saith the Lord . . . thoughts of peace, and not of evil . . . to give you an expected end. Then shall ye call upon me . . . and ye shall go . . . and pray unto me . . . and I will hearken unto you."

"Sounds like the Almighty is givin' you a message."

Austin looked up at the sky. "Well, I'm a-callin' on ya, Lord." He stuffed the holy book into his back pocket. "Lord, carry me somewhere outta here."

"You is goin' somewhere special. Wish I could go with you, that's all." Chuck shook Austin's hand.

Encouraged, he said, "And let me take Jeanette with me, then give us a little girl. I'm gonna write the Lord a letter, tellin' Him my dreams."

"Tell me when He sends one back to ya."

"I will." Mrs. Thompson could help him write his letter to God. Working on his father's peanut farm, he'd never had an opportunity to learn the proper structure of the English language. Yet the world would still hold him accountable for his lack of education and judge him because of his Southern dialect.

In regard to God's judgment of his prayers, Mrs. Thompson had said that the Almighty read a man's heart, so Austin hoped that the good Lord could ignore his botched English.

"Chuck."

"Make it quick, almost our turn."

"I wanna be a pastor."

"You're an ex-con. Ain't no church gonna hire you, Austin."

"Especially someone who don't speak good English." He bit his lower lip to keep it from trembling. Hoping for divine intervention into his plight, Austin dared a glance into the pink-and-purple watercolor sky. The heavens didn't rain down any answers.

"Sorry, friend. In spite of your past, I shouldn't of discouraged ya. Until the Almighty takes you where you're going, go on wit yo bad self."

The line toward the bank table crawled forward. Austin hadn't noticed it before, but a straw hat shaded the boss's pockmarked red face. Johnny, a field hand whose old blackened skin sagged off a skeleton of lanky bones, shuffled forward. Austin and Chuck followed.

Nervously, Chuck tapped his hand on the side of his thigh as Johnny received his pay. "Austin, tell me your rank in the Navy."

"Seaman."

"Important?" Chuck raised his chin.

"Not really."

"Don't short yourself, man."

"I'm bein' honest. Wasn't an officer or nothin' like that."

"Don't need no officer, unless there's seamen to lead."

"Made your point."

"I'm parched. Tell me 'bout the lemonade."

"We got time?"

"After we get paid."

The foreman counted, and Austin listened. "One, two, three . . ." All the way to thirty-five. Austin had never heard the foreman count past thirty-five.

"Name?" the foreman asked.

"Austin." He rubbed his arm across his forehead, perspiration slicking his skin.

"One, two . . . thirty-five, thirty-six, thirty-seven, and thirty-eight."

He grinned wide and stood taller. He wouldn't need to ask Jeanette and his baby girl to do without the finer things in life, like milk, eggs, and lemonade. They wouldn't be eating peanut butter like he ate for dinner every night.

The boss removed his straw hat. "Boy, you're outpickin' them all. You gonna bankrupt me, taking food from my chilluns' mouths."

Austin tucked his chin and backed away. *Boy*—the word flogged his pride. "Ain't no boy could do what I just done," he whispered beneath the rustling of the oak tree. Burying his hand in his pocket, he verified that the pocket was hole-free before releasing his week's salary.

"Thirty-eight dollars, man, you rich and ready for that

family," Chuck said, and then approached the bank table. After receiving his thirty-four dollars, he joined Austin. "Thirty-eight dollars, you and the lucky missus gonna be rich."

"What about schoolin' for my little girl?"

"Leave them type of questions for the Almighty and the preacher. Tell me 'bout the lemonade."

"If you want." The men walked shoulder to shoulder, slightly hunched from the day's labor. "At my pappy's peanut farm, my first tastes of life were sour. Barely enough food, and the white store owners never paid him a fair price for a crop of peanuts."

"Didn't treat my daddy no different. I understand."

"How's a man supposed to save a bit and send the kids to school?"

"You ain't. America ain't gonna give you nuthin', better ask the Almighty if you want anything. What 'bout your momma?"

"She died of drinkin' too much."

"Ms. Rosa Lee—the good Christian woman?"

"Naw. Rosa Lee wasn't my birth mother." He paused. "I always thought she drank to nurse a heart diseased with broken dreams."

"The devil's in the liquor, that's a fact."

"I saw the devil at sixteen years old."

"Where?"

"Hovering over my momma when I found her facedown in her own vomit."

"Whatcha do then?"

"Ran—lied about my age and enlisted in the United States Navy." Austin adjusted his stride, walking like a sailor.

"You never told me that back when we used to hang out at the juke joint."

"Didn't have the guts."

"Amazing what a man learns 'bout his friend in a day's work." Chuck put his arm around Austin's shoulder. "I'm proud of you, service and all."

"Thanks."

"How 'bout the Navy, sweet or sour?"

"Sweet at first, but the sour crept up on me."

"They weren't gonna treat no black man the same," Chuck said. "I could've told you that."

"It was worse."

"What'd they do to you?"

Austin shook his head. "I learned to tolerate the white man's injustice. It's what I did to myself."

"Don't leave me hangin'. You know I hate it when you do."

"You see, I was hurtin' so bad." He raised his hand to his chest. "On the inside."

"I ain't no stranger to hurtin'."

"I finished myself off."

"Whatcha mean?"

"Liquor—too much of it."

Chuck looked down at the ground. "I'm sorry, friend. I didn't know. Thought you'd gone off to live with your aunt. That's what your brother said when I came lookin' for ya."

"How could a jug of rotten corn render a man so stupid?"

"I ain't no scientist."

"Neither am I, but I drowned my dreams in a river of booze. They kicked me out of the Navy."

"Dishonorable discharge?"

Austin nodded. He peeked at his friend and then quickly at the ground again. "Cut my dreams real short of travelin', explorin', and havin' an honorable job."

"You was hopin' to find yourself a woman and have a baby girl."

"Wanted her to be a teacher, a scientist, or one of those dirt diggers who uncover ancient stuff."

"You mean an archaeologist?"

"One of those. Wanted someone real smart. She'd help me speak right, I know it."

"You can still find her. Sounds like you already did."

"I'm startin' to not believe it. Jeanette's smart. What would she want with me—an ex-con and fired sailor?"

"What happened after the Navy?"

"In and out of trouble. In and out of jobs. Homeless. Got into a fight in a juke joint. Man pulled a knife. I pulled a pistol from my pocket and shot him in the chest. Fifteen years in the state pen and now I'm here."

"But you survived."

"More like changed."

"How?"

"A carpenter came for a visit inside my prison cell. Momma told me I needed that man years ago, but I couldn't trust no white man grinnin' at me in all those church pictures."

"You mean Jesus? He ain't no white man."

"What about the pictures?"

"Jesus was a Jewish man."

"How does a Jew look?"

"All different kinds of ways—white, tan, and black." Chuck crossed his arms. "Jesus likes us too."

"Man, He loves us. That's what Chap Max Jones kept telling me till I got transformed."

"Details, man." Chuck ran in front of Austin, eager to hear more.

"1966, barely a year ago, I was sittin' on a thin cot behind steel bars wearing my chain-gang uniform—black stripes and all. I'd gone back to my concrete cell after a long day's work on the chain gang."

"If the man pulled a knife on you and you pulled a gun, how come that ain't self-defense?"

Austin waited, looking at his friend.

Chuck came to his own conclusions. "A black man in the South at the wrong place at the wrong time who killed someone was gonna do time if the victim looked black—and die if the victim passed for white."

Austin shrugged, wishing to forget. "On October 3, 1966, Santa Claus came to my prison cell."

"Santa Claus. You believe in that old joker?"

"Chap Max Jones looked like Santa with his snow-white hair."

"Cherry cheeks and all?"

"Yep, and as friendly. Man, I felt good after he talked at me—hopeful my life could be better. He talked to me with respect, like I was a somebody."

"You are. What'd he say?"

"Told me 'bout a carpenter who loved everybody no matter what color they were or what they'd done, and said this carpenter could erase my past and give me a new life."

"How's some carpenter gonna do that?"

"Chap Max called the carpenter Jesus—the guy who forgives us and cleans up all our messes."

"Momma always talked about Him, but I ain't never known He worked as a carpenter. Not much better than you and me."

"I needed some help, so since the carpenter was askin' for followers, I signed up. After that I started feelin' clean, could hold my head up a little bit."

"I'm still stuck on a white man stoppin' to reach through prison bars to help a black man."

"Man, Chap Max was different, smilin' all the time."

"I ain't convinced. What'd he want from you?"

"You ain't ready yet. When you are, won't take no convincin'."

Chuck and Austin stopped at the fork in the road. Austin removed his soaked shirt and slung the threadbare garment across his shoulder.

"Nice talkin' to you, Austin." Chuck shook his friend's hand.

"Don't let no one keep you from the carpenter's love. He don't like the red over the yellow rose. Matter of fact, He's probably color-blind like me."

"Thanks, my friend. See ya in the fields on Monday. May see ya at the old church house on Sunday."

"I'd like that. Introduce you to Jeanette and serve you up a glass of Mrs. Thompson's lemonade."

Chuck walked down his fork in the road and disappeared into the distance. After watching his friend turn the last bend toward his house, Austin stared down the path that loomed ahead. The five-mile walk wouldn't get done standing there, so he started walking, thinking about Gus and hoping he was okay.

One stop remained before going home—the grocery store. *Lord, let the owner be in a happy mood. Let him give me a fair price.* After twenty minutes of walking, Austin pushed the glass door open. A bell chimed. The store owner looked up and quickly went back to his own business.

"How you doin', sir?" Austin trudged toward a loaf of wheat bread. The owner nodded.

"Don't steal that, boy. I'll have the hounds on your tail so fast . . ." The store owner allowed Austin to finish the sentence in his imagination.

Lord, take me to a place where there ain't no threats for a man takin' his hard-earned money to buy a loaf of bread. Keeping his eyes down, he placed a jar of peanut butter and the loaf of bread on the counter. He'd go fishing in Lake Okeechobee next Saturday and bring home some fish for him and Gus.

"Two dollars."

Austin gulped down a protest. The first time he'd objected, the store owner had doubled the price to four dollars, taking almost all of Austin's daily pay. He handed the man two dollars, grabbed his dinner, and left the store, heading for his one-room shanty.

Home. Austin inhaled scents of the swamp and smiled.

4—GUS

6:00 P.M.
FRIDAY, AUGUST 11, 1967
BELLE GLADE, FLORIDA

A CLUTCH OF BISMARCK PALMS and pine trees hid Austin's shanty. Tired of sleeping in the boss's overcrowded bunk housing, Austin had saved a week's wages, hauled off some old wood from Old Man Smith's farm, and built the one-room shack. Shack or not, it belonged to him, and that meant that he owned a home.

He lifted the wooden latch. The rickety door protested with a squeak. A thin yellow lab lumbered toward him, arthritis slowing his gait. Water dripped off the dog, matting down the graying fur around his black nose.

"Gus, you been swimming again?" He must have escaped from the hole in the back of the shack. Austin's patch of branches and leaves hadn't deterred the dog's hunting.

Gus nudged his owner with his muzzle, and Austin leaned down and patted his companion's head. "Let's go explorin' tonight."

The dog wagged his tail, thumping the wall of the shanty.

"Be careful, ol' yeller. Don't knock down our house with your tail."

Gus sat, waiting for his master's direction. Austin left the door open. Inside, he unclasped a rolled-up net. The net hung in the doorway, keeping the bugs out but allowing a little air to filter through and cool things down.

"Brought us home a sandwich." Austin opened his grocery bag and placed the contents on a makeshift table. He opened the jar, dipped in a clean spoon, and prepared two peanut butter sandwiches. He took a bite out of one and gave the other to Gus. While eating, he read his collection of old newspapers. Mrs. Thompson had a habit of donating a week's worth of papers to him on Sunday. "You must keep up with your reading lessons," she'd say.

After dinner, Austin slung a dry towel over his shoulder, gathered a bundle of fresh clothes, and picked up a piece of soap. He pushed back the net and headed to a shallow creek for a bath. Gus followed.

At the creek bank, he yanked a dead palm branch from the ground and laid it on the shore. He slipped off his work clothes, washed them in the little stream, and then laid them on the branch. Gus's tail wagged.

Austin stepped into the water. The cool liquid lapped his gritty skin.

His dog bolted in behind him, splashing and playing in the creek.

"Gus, watch out for them gators and moccasins."

The aging mutt splashed harder.

After bathing, Austin dressed in his explorer's outfit: a pair of tan dungarees, a green cotton shirt, and the same pair of shoes. *Time to go dirt digging—or archaeology shovelin', as Chuck had put it—and sell my treasures to the highest bidder.*

With his tail wagging, Gus followed his master up the stream.

"You imagine we're gonna find an ancient Indian treasure in that swamp cabbage? It'd put my baby girl through college."

Gus tilted his head as though he understood. The dog had been trained not to bark unless danger was imminent, so he kept his thoughts to himself.

Crickets chirped through the silent field. Private, the way Austin liked it. No neighbors to ask a question and judge his answer. Only the bugs, snakes, and gators, and they were too busy surviving to judge.

Gus whined.

"You're tired, old boy. Let's head back. Almost time for Friday night's gospel church-sing."

Gus's ears stood at attention.

Stopping, Austin listened.

Leaves rustled in the cool evening breeze, almost masking the menacing sound—like two dry peas knocking up against the sides of a tin cup, only quieter.

"Don't see it, Gus."

Back arched, the dog didn't move.

"She sure knows we're here." Austin scanned the underbrush.

A creature with black diamond scales launched out from beneath a swamp cabbage and bit Gus's leg.

"Gus!" Austin unearthed a stone. Dazed with a father's protective anger, he bludgeoned the serpent, attempting to decapitate it.

After releasing Gus's leg, the rattlesnake prepared for another strike while continuing to sound its warning.

Austin lunged forward, crushing the snake's head with the rock.

The snake writhed back and forth, fighting to sink its fangs into Austin's skin. Determined, he ground the stone into the dirt until the writhing abated. "You devil!"

Gus lay on the ground, his aging body already weakened. The old boy drooled and panted. Austin lifted the dog and ran back to his shanty. "There ain't no dog doctor, just me and you, ol' Gus. No different than when I first found you by ol' man Potter's ditch—all eaten up with fleas."

With mournful eyes, Gus stared up at his master and whined.

He pushed the screen back, entered their home, and laid the dog across their bed—some old wooden pallets covered with sheets and a worn-out bedspread.

"Don't die on me. You're all I got right now. I know you're getting old, but hang in there."

5—Monday Mornin'

ON MONDAY MORNING, FROGS SANG in the distance.

Silvery specks of the bright moon's glow tunneled through the slats of Austin's shack. An orange flame flickered atop melting candle wax, casting a tawny illumination across his shanty.

Austin palmed Gus's head as the dog lay on their makeshift bed.

His right back leg muscles had turned into black mush, and pus oozed. The dog shook with fine tremors that never stopped. Austin covered his four-legged friend with another blanket, hoping to staunch his companion's shaking and panting, and then exited their home. A potion bubbled in a tin pot outside; he removed it from the stove, set it on the ground to cool, and reentered the shack to check on Gus.

Minutes later, Austin applied another hot compress of liquefied burdock roots to Gus's leg. "You're okay. Gonna take good care of you. I ain't leavin' you, no matter what."

As he laid another rag across Gus's leg, the dog barely moved. He hadn't eaten a peanut butter sandwich in more than twenty-four hours, so Austin poured drops of cool water down his companion's throat.

Dazed, Austin hadn't slept since Friday night, and Sunday morning church service had come and gone. Afraid that Gus would die alone, Austin hadn't gone anywhere.

"The boss is gonna fire me if I skip work. I'm needin' you to go on and get better." He massaged Gus's still body. "Lord, what do I do?" he cried out. "Help me. Help me, Lord. Chuck was right, the wantin' ain't never gonna stop."

6—TIBET

ANSWERS TO PRAYERS OFTEN SURPRISE.

Gus lay perfectly still.

No more writhing, shaking, or panting—or breathing, for that matter.

Austin's companion had died, and the only thing left to do was to bury him. The sun hadn't yet peeked through the trees. He looked at the face of his watch—2:17 a.m.

After wrapping Gus in a sheet, Austin carried the dog outside. Gus had always loved the stream, and as far as Austin knew, no one relied upon the shallow bubbling brook for a source of clean water. He'd always drawn water from an abandoned well near his shack. So five feet from the water's edge, he started digging with the same shovel he'd used to dig the foundation of his dirt-floor shack.

After forty minutes, he patted the dirt over the top of the dog's tomb.

In the distance, something pale bobbed atop the flowing stream.

Austin crept to the shore and waited. His breath stopped in his chest. "That's a baby. A dead baby. What in heaven's name?" If the law caught a colored man with a white baby, it'd be his neck. He slid his hands around his neck and squeezed for emphasis.

As he watched, the tiny corpse floated past. "Oh God, don't hold it against me for doing nothing. You don't understand how it is down here." A cold sweat crept down his face and soaked through his shirt.

Another thirty minutes passed, and Austin left the gravesite and returned to his hut, Gus and that tiny baby haunting him. Sleep-deprived from the last forty-eight hours of nursing, he couldn't imagine toiling and harvesting sugarcane beneath Florida's hot sun for twelve hours.

Austin ached, deep and to the bone. It had as much to do with the loss of his friend as the loss of sleep. And the dead baby—oh Lord, he couldn't think about it. Loneliness followed close behind the ache. From now on, he'd be coming home to no one. Alone. He sat on the edge of his bed and buried his face in his hands.

"Lord, I can't go back to them fields. No sir, I can't. Help me. Maybe I ain't supposed to be wantin' nothin' more than what I got," his voice broke, "but a man's gotta have dreams. You give me a baby girl like you gave childless Hannah, and I'll give my little one back to you. She won't be floatin' down no backwater pond. She's yours. Promise. I'll borrow her from time to time, but leave the missus with me. Can we work something out?"

A whistle pierced the rustle of leaves outside Austin's shack, stopping his heart cold. Nobody knew he lived here. Had the whistling man witnessed Austin's refusal to help the infant? How does one help a dead baby?

"Austin, you in there?" The sound of halting, rolling consonants and vowels sounded familiar.

"Is that you, Tibet?"

"It's me, man." The old Jamaican with weathered black skin pulled back the net.

"What you sneakin' up on a man for?"

"Ol' Gus gone?" Tibet pointed at Austin's dirty shovel.

"Buried him by the river."

"Sorry 'bout that."

Austin stepped forward. "How'd you know my dog's name?"

"Somebody told me." Smiling, Tibet looked up at the sky. Beneath a full moon, his teeth were no longer dingy but sparkled white. "If-f-f love's a fish, she must be a pink salmon, swimmin' up a cold-water creek—troubled, tryin' somethin' mighty to find her intended."

"That's my line—I ain't never told you . . ."

"Somebody did." He glanced back up at the ceiling as though he was waiting for a spaceship to land. "Not too many parents dedicate their child to a higher purpose before they're even conceived. Bold promise, Austin."

"How'd you know?"

"Man, I keep telling you, somebody told me. You gonna keep your promise?"

"I'm a man of my word."

"The Way-Maker could work something out. Do you want an answer to your prayer or were you just talking, man?"

"An answer." Austin mustered up every bit of fortitude to hide the trembling of his body as Tibet dug into his pocket and removed a plum velvet box.

"Give it to your daughter on her thirteenth birthday."

"I ain't even married."

"And you don't have a woman. Details." Tibet laughed. "Don't give it to her until she's thirteen, and never forget that *you* asked for this."

"Understood." Austin shifted his weight. "Hey, Tibet. I . . . I saw a dead baby. I didn't do it. Promise."

"I know. Some crazy man drowned him up the river." Tibet's eyes lightened from black to violet. Shocked, Austin stepped back, slamming his back into the doorframe of his shanty. Tibet rested his hand on his friend's shoulder. "You've got to understand, man. Some humans are so determined to kill, there is no heavenly intervention. But the baby rests in heaven's bosom, and we'll care for him."

"We'll care for him . . . who's *we*?"

"Don't worry, man." Tibet pressed his hand into Austin's chest. "You possess the heart of a father." Then, as if the air could absorb humans, Tibet disappeared. Austin reached for the Jamaican, but his grasp clasped empty air. *Be not forgetful to entertain strangers . . . for thereby some have entertained angels unawares.*

"My little girl's gonna need a friend—a friend who's a girl."

7—Maps and Lemonade

EXCEEDINGLY AND ABUNDANTLY ABOVE ALL we can ask or think—dreams do come true.

"Daddy's home!" Daniela Cavanaugh bounded from her mother's lap and burst past the door into her daddy's arms.

"How's Daddy's little girl?" Chaplain Austin Cavanaugh lifted his four-year-old daughter into the air. He was strong and well nourished; Jeanette's home-cooked meals and endless glasses of lemonade had done the trick.

"I'm just fine, thank you." She swung her long black pigtails, ends clasped with pink barrettes, around her head.

"You speak like a little lady."

"I've been teaching her." Jeanette smiled and kissed her husband of five years. Everything had a time and a place.

Chaplain Max Jones had introduced Austin to the founder of an alcohol rehabilitation center—Dunklin Memorial Camp in Okeechobee, Florida. After seminary training, Austin was ordained a minister and worked for Chaplain Max at Florida State Prison in Raiford. On the weekends, he attended revival camp meetings through-out southern Florida. One night, he ran into Jeanette at a camp meeting in Okeechobee. They married three months later.

"What do you want to be when you grow up?" He tugged on one of Daniela's pigtails.

"A doctor who helps sick patients, so they can get better. Guess what, Daddy?"

"What?"

"Mommy and I went digging in the backyard."

"Daniela, that's called archaeology." Her mother smiled and pulled her little girl into her embrace. "Let me braid the rest of your hair."

"An archaeologist, a doctor, and an astronaut." Austin knelt down and faced his daughter, holding her petite hands while her mother combed through her thick hair. "You're smart and beautiful, just like your mother."

"And pretty darn determined, like her father. Just look at what you've accomplished—and how much your Eng-lish has improved."

"I've been studying every day. I couldn't imagine giving a bad example to our little one." Austin was enraptured as his gaze followed Daniela's every move.

"Daddy . . ." Daniela reached up and touched her father's cheek.

If Austin had been made of ice, he would have melted beneath his daughter's touch. "Yes, darling?"

"I want a friend, like Mr. Chuck was to you."

"He was one of the best, Danny." Austin slid from in front of the mirror and looked at the reflection of his daughter and his wife. "I'm sure the Almighty will gift you the best friend a little girl could want. Wait and see."

"Will she have pigtails like mine?"

"Of course. And just as pretty."

After finishing the last braid, his wife moved away from the mirror. It was aged and the silver on the back of the glass had oxidized, resulting in a leopard's coat of black spots.

"Where's this mirror from, Mommy?"

"My grandmother gave it to my mother."

"Why is there a tall man standing behind me in it?"

Austin's heart raced. He glanced into the empty air behind his daughter and then back to the foggy mirror. Embracing his daughter, he said, "I don't see anyone, sweetie."

"I do. He's tall, and sometimes he glows like your wedding band. He has wings down to his feet."

Austin kept his hand at his side and rotated the gold band around his fourth finger.

"Other times, he's almost as black as Mommy's iron skillet. His teeth are always shiny white when he smiles." Daniela waved into the mirror. "Hi, Mister. Why don't you come out so Mommy and Daddy can see you?" She looked at her daddy. "He doesn't want to come. He doesn't want to be my friend like Mr. Chuck is yours." She swiped at her eyes.

"It's okay, my love." Austin stroked her back as Jeanette disappeared into the kitchen. *In a few minutes, she'll bring lemonade for all of us—that'll cheer up my Danny Rose, my Orphan Dreamer.* "Your friend will come, wait and see. Maybe she's lost inside a castle on the other side of the world." He kissed Daniela on the cheek.

"Let's send her a map, okay?"

"Lemonade, everyone?" Jeanette carried a tray of the sweet beverages, the pale yellow liquid swirling and dipping through ice in tall glasses.

Quietly, Austin asked Jeanette, "The man in the mirror—do you think he's Danny's protector?"

"Why do I need a protector?"

The child has better hearing than old Gus did. Austin's tongue stuck to the roof of his mouth. He swigged down a mouthful of lemonade. "We all need angels."

* * *

Daniela sipped on her lemonade.

Daniela.

"Yes, Daddy?"

"I didn't call you."

"I thought you did."

Daniela.

"Yes, Daddy. You called me."

"No. I didn't."

"Are you playing tricks on me?" Daniela snuggled by her father on the couch.

Her father reached for her mother's hand. "Next time

you hear someone call your name, respond 'Here I am, Yeshua.'"

"Yes, Daddy."

Later that night, Daniela rolled out of her bed to use the restroom. She turned on the bathroom light. A shadow flew past the vanity mirror. She gasped, ran back into her bedroom, and hid beneath the covers.

Daniela.

She remembered her dad's instructions. "H-h-here I am," she whispered.

"I love you, Daniela Rose. Follow Me."

"Okay, Yeshua. You can be my line leader." She got up and followed the Master—the Great I AM. "Where are we going? To find my bosom friend like Mister Chuck?"

On an adventure . . .

Dear Reader,

A title oftentimes allows the reader to start falling in love with a story before reading the first word. I love the title of my second novelette, birthed from the backstories of characters in the Orphan Dreamer Series, originally named The God Factor Saga (GFS).

"A Generation of Lighted Evergreens" is rather special to me because it tells a snippet of my late father's real-life journey. I have fictionalized some parts for dramatic purposes, but the overall theme of divine second changes rings true. I hope this short story resonates deep within your soul, as it did mine.

So, what themes shine through the title?

"Lighted Evergreens"—representing the sacrificial love of the Light of the Universe as He continues to shine through the world's darkness, casting a beacon of illumination for all who are willing to follow His simple message of compassion. Yeshua (the Hebrew name for Jesus) is truly an evergreen, blooming with unconditional love throughout life's ever-changing seasons. Strong, He towers above frail humanity, splitting time in two—BC and AD—our turning point in history, the year of our Lord. Compassionate, He stoops low, offering second chances to the repentant and uplifting the humble.

"A Generation"—representing a father's love for his treasured daughter. Join me as we discover Austin Cavanaugh's love for his daughter, Daniela—a young girl whose purpose will change the world, one generation at a time.

The Orphan Dreamer Saga (ODS) is a serialized seven-book story about ordinary people with purpose. Each character can choose to be infused with Yeshua's compassion, but when they choose to follow the Master, they must sacrifice their plans and take up Yeshua's cross to follow Him. If you'd like to continue reading the ODS, I recommend following the book guide at the end of this novelette. The first novel in the saga is *Orphan Dreamer and The Glass Tattoo*.

Please find updates on my website, www.JNellBrown.com, or on my Facebook page. As always, when my pen strokes the page, I'm writing for the One, for when I couldn't walk, He carried me.

Blessings,
J. Nell Brown

"A Generation of Lighted Evergreens" is dedicated to my late father, Chaplain Austin Brown, a man with lowly beginnings whom God lifted up, allowing him to travel the world and share Yeshua's love with dignitaries and inmates alike, not discriminating between the rich or poor.

This novelette is also dedicated to my mother, Mrs. Jeanette Brown, a woman of purpose, sacrificial love, and resolute faith.

Acknowledgments

Yeshua, thank you for inspiring this book through my imagination at a time when I needed it most. You've always been faithful to me.

Special thanks to my late father, Chaplain Austin Brown; my mother, Mrs. Jeanette Brown; and my sisters and friends.

To my editors, Ann Castro and Emily Dings at AnnCastro Studio, Faralee Pozo at Upwork.com, and Courtney Rae Andersson at Elevation Editorial—thank you all for your eagle-eye talents.

To my readers, thank you for loving this story. These characters exist for you.

Dear Reader,

Thoughtful Amazon reviews about an author's work are like a pay raise or a tip to employees in traditional jobs. If you enjoyed this short story, "A Generation of Lighted Evergreens," please take a moment to place a review on Amazon.com, sharing with other readers what you've learned. Your feedback is invaluable.

The A21 Campaign, a nonprofit organization to abolish the human trafficking of children, is my charity of choice. When you purchase a short story or novel in the Orphan Dreamer saga, 10 percent of the profits will be donated to A21 Campaign.

I look forward to saying *hello* to you on Facebook. Please like my page so you can keep up with the writing journey. Also, please sign up for my newsletter, and I will notify you about future releases, sales and special events.

With gratitude,
J. Nell Brown

Author Biography

J. Nell Brown, the daughter of a chaplain and a teacher, is a Florida native.

Her relationship with Yeshua (Jesus) is fused with experiences in life, travel, extensive Bible study, and people's stories, and she combines all of this to create characters, plots, and settings for her novels and short stories. An involuntary insomniac, Brown practices medicine and writes in her free time.

She is a self-proclaimed nerd and loves all things scientific. Her love of science is demonstrated by her research at Los Alamos National Laboratory, the site for the development of the atomic bomb. She graduated with honors from the University of Florida (U of F) College of Agriculture and received her medical doctorate from the same.

After completing an anesthesia residency at The University of Chicago Hospitals, she practices in Florida.

Her heart overflows with compassion for hurting people, particularly children. A portion of the proceeds from this book will go to the A21 Campaign, a rescue charity for human-trafficked children, and Eastside Baptist School in Gainesville, Florida, a school of love, values, and solid educational curriculum for children whose parents would not otherwise be able to afford an alternative school education.

Her first nonfiction book, *Shhh, My Father Is Speaking, and I Am Listening,* is about her prayer journey. The Bible is her favorite literary masterpiece. You may follow J. Nell Brown on her author website, JNellBrown.com.

HouseGuest

I

Immortals Time Without End

I'M IN A COLD CAVE, which is rather ironic because I'm in hell.

Tsk. Tsk. Don't pity me. After the moon drips with blood, I will come for you. Until then, I'm here at my summer residence, prepping for our meeting—Armageddon, the day I scrub Earth clean of its invaders.

You.

My most treasured possession sits beside me while humans squint, then peek through the optics of a telescope only to ask, "Is there an intelligent life form in outer space?" I laugh. Only a nitwit and self-centered creature would look into a telescope and ask such a stupid question. If a creature requires a telescope to see me, they are working at a disadvantage.

I see you.

Here's looking at you, kid. No optics. No lens. No convex shiny mirrors. No telescope. And now it's my turn to ask, "Does any intelligent life exist on Earth?"

I already know the answer: No, not yet. But very soon. I look down past Earth's atmosphere. The moon is full. Bright. White. One day it will darken to blood red at the right time. Then, we will come back, and there will only be enough room for one species—mine.

"Welcome home, Nomed," I say to myself, eager for the day when Aglaope whispers these three words into my ear as we stand side by side on the sugary-white beaches of Key West, Florida, or the snow-packed ridges of Mount Everest. I love the cold. It suits me.

"You're in good practice." Aglaope smiles at me.

"I'm ready. No. *We're* ready to return home, Agla." I gaze into the distance. Cloaked in secrecy, my winter home approaches Earth. Ah, when a plan comes together!

We call our Trojan horse Wormwood. Larger than the sun, the invisible planet hides in the shadows of Earth's universe, deep in a wormhole that no human has dared to explore. Besides, the inky black entrance into that wormhole appears as a tiny speck through Earth's most powerful telescopes. My warriors train day and night in preparation for our day of reckoning—the day we invade Earth and take it back, making the planet great once again.

"When they see Wormwood, it will be too late, Agla."

"And that's why you're his general, Nomed. Cunning.

Ruthless. Decisive." Her left eye scarred shut, Aglaope gazes into my left eye. "Could a human fight your warriors and win?"

"Of course."

"But you promised me!" She pulls away from my embrace. "You promised that all would be well. That I would be safe."

"They could win if they knew how to fight us. But they don't know how to fight us, and their bullets, nuclear warheads, aircraft carriers, and submarines will be useless in this fight. They will kill themselves. But not us. Never fear. Humans couldn't figure out how to give life if they tried. How long have they played around in the most prestigious laboratories, yet not cured cancer?"

"This weapon . . ." Aglaope reaches for my hand. "What is it?"

"I hold this secret closer to my bosom than I have held you."

"Nomed, tell me," she whines.

"No! It's for your protection, my love. Do not ask me again."

9 781942 849148